# Charlie and Biff

## Margaret Ryan and Wendy Smith

**Young Lions**

## JUMBO JETS

**Forecast of Fear** · Keith Brumpton
**Pickles Sniffs it Out** · Michaela Morgan
**Bernie Works a Miracle** · Leon Rosselson
**Fergus the Forgetful** ·
**Charlie and Biff** · Margaret Ryan
**The Man in Shades** · Pat Thomson
**Sir Quinton Quest Hunts the Yeti** ·
**Sir Quinton Quest Hunts the Jewel** ·
Kaye Umansky

First published in Great Britain by
A&C Black (Publishers) Ltd 1994
First published in Young Lions 1994

10 9 8 7 6 5 4 3 2 1

Young Lions is an imprint of the Children's Division,
part of HarperCollins Publishers Ltd,
77-85 Fulham Palace Road, London W6 8JB

Text copyright © 1994 Margaret Ryan
Illustrations copyright © 1994 Wendy Smith
All rights reserved.
ISBN 0 00 675006-0

Printed and bound in Great Britain by
HarperCollins Manufacturing Glasgow

# CHAPTER ONE
*Charlie and Biff*

It was Wednesday afternoon in room three of Grey Towers primary school, and time for the art lesson.

My favourite lesson of the week. I wish it could be Art every day, instead of sums. I wish I didn't have to do sums ever again.

I wish you would hand out those palettes instead of daydreaming Charlie, or we'll never get on with the art lesson.

Yes, Miss Allison.

Charlie was good at Art, not bad at English and rotten at sums, so his last school report had said. It also said he could be slow and dreamy and that he spent too much time gazing out of the window.

Charlie finished handing out the palettes, and settled down to listen to the art lesson. It was very interesting. All about self-portraits.

Charlie looked. His face looked back, and
Charlie drew what he saw.

Beside him, Marilyn Marchmont drew a
pale pink face surrounded by long blonde
hair. On his other side, Lenny Steadman
drew a round brown face with a huge
smiley grin.

Charlie grinned back at it. He couldn't
help it. It was that kind of picture.

Then Charlie looked back at his own
portrait, and his grin faded.

Then some drops of water dripped down on to Charlie's head, rolled down his real nose and dripped on to the portrait, washing away the freckles on his painted cheeks as well.

Next morning, at assembly in the school hall, while Charlie was gazing out of the window at a small robin lugging a huge worm across the grass, there was a special announcement.

'Grey Towers primary school,' said Mrs Tait, the head teacher, 'is falling down.

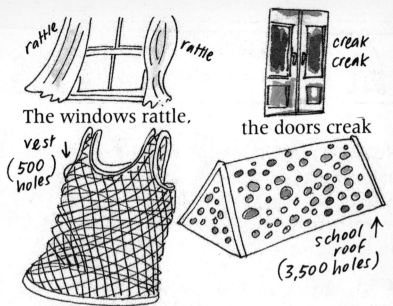

rattle
rattle

The windows rattle,

creak
creak

the doors creak

vest (500 holes) →

school roof ↑ (3,500 holes)

and the roof has more holes in it than a string vest. I've phoned Mr Snodgrass at the School Buildings' Department yet again, to ask what's to be done about it, and he told me that Grey Towers school may soon be closed down.'

SNEAKY SNODDERS

o
o
plip

What's to be done about the roof?

o plop

HEADMASTER

It's probably not worth doing anything. Grey Towers school may soon be closed down.

There was a startled gasp throughout the hall.

11

volunteered Charlie.

chorused the school.

That day, there was talk of nothing else but the fete, and the fight to save the school.

'I'll ask my mum to help me bake a huge fruit cake, and people can pay twenty pence to guess the weight,' said Marilyn.

'I'll ask my mum to help me make meringues,' said Lenny. 'Everyone likes them. They're bound to sell well.'

Charlie nodded, but didn't say anything. He lived with his dad, who wasn't any good at making fruit cakes or meringues. Not that he hadn't tried.

# CHAPTER THREE
*A wonderful idea*

That afternoon, instead of dawdling along the pavement, gazing at the cracks, Charlie raced home and told the whole story to his dog, Biff.

Biff was large and hairy and was called Biff because he always biffed Charlie with his nose to attract his attention.

What I need Biff, is a really knock-out idea for the school fete. Something that no one else has thought of. Something that I can organise by myself. Something that's really going to attract the crowds.

Biff nodded his scruffy head, stuck out his big pink tongue, and panted, 'HEH HEH HEH HEH HEH.' He put his head on one side for a moment then biffed Charlie with his nose, and began parading up and down, lifting his big hairy paws neatly off the floor as he went.

HEH
HEH
HEH

'Okay okay, relax. I'll take you out in a minute, Biff. Can't you see I'm busy thinking?'

But Biff biffed Charlie again and began parading up and down once more, this time lifting his big hairy paws even higher.

But instead of running to the door as he usually did when he heard the word 'walk', Biff tossed his scruffy head in the air as though he was a fine stallion, and broke into a mincing trot up and down the sitting room carpet.

Charlie stopped dead and gaped at Biff.

'I've got it. I've got it,' he yelled. 'I've got a great idea for the school fete. A PETS' PARADE. I could organise a PETS' PARADE, and charge everybody a pound to enter their pet. That's bound to bring in a lot of money. Wow, what a wonderful idea.

You're a genius, Biff. I'm a genius. Just wait till I tell everyone my idea tomorrow. This school fete's going to be fantastic.'

# CHAPTER FOUR
*What about Dad?*

Everyone in school thought a pets' parade was a great idea.

When Charlie heard the word DRAW, his brain went into overdrive.

Charlie raced home that day, and told his dad all about his ideas, and about what everyone else was doing for the fete.

20

The next day, something did. During morning break, Charlie told Lenny about his dad. Lenny told his mum.

That evening, Lenny's mum turned up at Charlie's house.

'Thanks very much, you're a great help,' said Mrs Steadman. 'Here's the recipe. I'll give you a call later in the week to see how you're getting on.' And she winked at Charlie and left!

Charlie and his dad looked at the recipe. It needed:

Mrs. Steadman's Chocolate Truffles

ONE PACKET OF DIGESTIVE BISCUITS
(crushed)
ONE TIN OF CONDENSED MILK
50g. DESSICATED COCONUT
50g. CHOCOLATE POWDER
150g. MARGARINE
VERMICELLI (for coating)

Looks good, Dad. Biff and I will go to the shops right away and get the ingredients. I can't wait to taste your chocolate truffles.

# CHAPTER FIVE
*Preparations*

The chocolate truffles were a great success. Mr Johnstone had telephoned Mrs Steadman several times to check the recipe.

Normal lessons were forgotten that week as Grey Towers primary school got ready for the fete. All the infants brought in their teddies for a teddy bears' picnic. Class two brought in their toys for a Good as New Sale. And Class three made up a special song:

Charlie spent the morning helping Mr Brown, the caretaker, to hang out some flags, and put up a big sign at the school gate that said:

GREY TOWERS PRIMARY SCHOOL
GRAND FETE
This Saturday
in aid of roof repairs
COME AND HELP SAVE
GREY TOWERS SCHOOL

Charlie was so busy that he didn't see a
big black car pull up outside the school
gate, and a man with a long nose and ears
to match wind down the car window,
peer at the sign and mutter to himself . . .

Nor did Charlie see a large black dog staring out of the back window as the car sped off, or the car's very unusual registration number SNE AK 1.

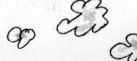

# CHAPTER SIX
*Sneaky Snodders*

Next day Charlie was kept busy making all the signs for the fete.

THIS WAY TO THE PETS' PARADE

FOLLOW THE HORSESHOES TO PIN THE TAIL ON THE DONKEY

THE TEDDY BEARS' PICNIC

He was so busy, he didn't even have time to gaze out of the classroom window. So he didn't see a big black car draw up, and a man with a long nose and ears to match get out, and enter the school.

'Ah, Mrs Tait,' said Mr Snodgrass, finding Mrs Tait on her hands and knees in the school hall, trying to fix a trestle-table that wouldn't stay up.

'You mean you're going to have it repaired after all?' beamed Mrs Tait, standing up so quickly the trestle-table collapsed again in a heap.

'You never keep them anyway,'
muttered Mrs Tait, as she led Mr
Snodgrass to see the worst of the damage.

Mr Snodgrass smiled nastily. 'Just YOU wait and see, Mrs Tait,' he muttered to himself as he left the school. 'I mean to have Grey Towers school, and as for this silly fete . . . I'll soon think of a way of ruining that.' Then he got into his car, slammed the car door shut, and roared off in a great cloud of smoke.

# CHAPTER SEVEN
*Even Sneakier Snodders*

After school that day, Charlie hurried along to see Mr Coats who owned the local pet shop.

Hallo, Charlie boy.

Hallo, Charlie. What'll it be today? More dog biscuits for Biff?

No thanks, Mr Coats. I'm organising a pets' parade for our school fete on Saturday and I came to ask if you'd judge the parade for us and hand out the prizes.

'YOU'RE organising the pets' parade, Charlie? Well I never. Of course I'll do the judging for you. I'd be delighted. I was coming along to the fete anyway. Got to keep the old school open. I went to that school, you know, and my brother Steve.'

'PC Coats?'

'That's right. He's on duty on Saturday, I'll ask him to look in. He never could resist Pin the Tail on the Donkey.'

Charlie handed Mr Coats a bit of paper. 'I've made a list of the three competitions people can enter their pets for: BEST-LOOKING PET, BEST-BEHAVED PET and CUDDLIEST PET.'

'You've certainly given this a lot of thought,' said Mr Coats, 'and since I'd like to help save the school too, I'll donate the prizes for the competitions. A month's food supply for the pets that win.'

37

# CHAPTER EIGHT
*Disaster!*

'Are you ready, Dad?' Charlie called to Mr Johnstone, who was putting on his anorak and juggling with five more boxes of chocolate truffles. Once he'd started making them he hadn't been able to stop.

It's time we were off to help set up all the stalls. I'm really looking forward to this fete.

Me too.

Charlie and his
dad were among the
first to arrive at the school.
Charlie tied Biff to a tree and took
out his sketch pad and pencil.
Mr Johnstone went over to help
Mrs Steadman set up the cake stall.

At two o'clock sharp, the school gates
opened and Grey Towers school fete
began. Charlie roamed around drawing
all that was happening.

He drew Miss Allison on the bric-a-brac
stall wrapping up a ghastly green vase for
a small boy. Then he drew the boy giving
the vase to his mother.

He drew Mrs. Tait drawing a clown's face
on Marilyn at the face-painting.

He drew Lenny pinning on the donkey's tail. On its left ear.

He looked around for Mr Coats and found him over at the home-baking stall, chatting to Dad.

Charlie untied Biff and went with Mr
Coats to where the judging was to be
held. Mr Coats looked along the line of
pets.

What a fine collection.
This is going to be a hard
job. I'd better take my jacket
off and put on my specs.

He carefully examined all the pets then
asked their owners to parade them up
and down.

When it was Biff's turn, he tossed his scruffy head as though he were a fine stallion then picked up his big hairy paws and minced up and down.

Everybody fell about laughing. Then the laughing stopped as a large black ownerless dog suddenly appeared from nowhere. Snarling and growling, the dog charged through the line of owners and pets, knocking them all over.

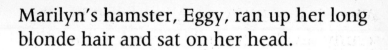

Marilyn's hamster, Eggy, ran up her long blonde hair and sat on her head.

Lenny's tortoise, Zippy, settled on Lenny's chest, and tucked himself in like a pie crust.

45

And Charlie tripped over Biff's big hairy legs and fell flat on his nose.

Then Biff and the other dogs took off after the large black dog. They went barging through the bric-a-brac.

They went trampling through the teddy bears' picnic.

They went hurtling through the home-
baking.

The big black dog who had
caused all the trouble
carried on right through
the middle of the
Pin the Tail on
the Donkey and
got clean away.

Only Biff kept doggedly after him, and
Charlie chasing after Biff SAW the large
black dog leap into a big black car driven
by a man with a long nose and ears to
match. And Charlie noticed the car had a
very unusual registration number.

Mrs Allison looked around in dismay.

Oh no, just look at the mess that dreadful dog has caused. The fete is ruined. We'll never make enough money to save the school now.

49

At that moment PC Coats arrived. He got out of his car and looked around in amazement.

'I'm glad you've arrived,' said Mr Coats. 'Perhaps you can help.' And he told his brother all that had happened.

Charlie took his sketch pad and pencil out of his pocket and started to draw.

'Why that's . . . ' said Mr Coats.

'Sneaky Snodders . . . Mr Snodgrass,' said Mrs Tait, 'the School Buildings' Inspector in charge of repairs. I'd know that nose and those ears anywhere.'

'But he comes into my shop,' said Mr Coats. 'Surely it couldn't be him . . .'

'What does he buy?' asked Charlie.

'Well . . . dog biscuits, mostly, or sometimes Good Boy chews . . . '

'Right,' said PC Coats. 'Time to do a little investigating. I'll go along and see him.'

'We'll ALL go along and see him,' said Mrs Tait. 'I wouldn't miss this for the world.'

Five minutes later they had arrived at Mr Snodgrass's house.

'Now I'll do the talking,' said PC Coats. 'Just leave it all to me.'

'Right,' said Charlie.

PC Coats rang the doorbell. After a few moments, Mr Snodgrass, alias Sneaky Snodders, came to the door.

Good afternoon INSPECTOR. Can I help you?

I'd like to ask you a few questions concerning an incident at Grey Towers primary school this afternoon when a large black dog ran through the school fete, causing considerable damage and great alarm.

Oh dear, how distressing. but how can I help?

Do you, sir, own a large black dog?

Yes, I do, but he's a real sweetie. Wouldn't hurt a fly.

What a fibber.

Cuddles sloped forward and sat down
with his tongue hanging out of one side
of his mouth.

'Just wait a moment,' said Mr Snodgrass. 'Before you accuse my dog of anything, have you got any evidence?'

'We have this drawing, Sir, done by this young lad, of the man who collected the aforementioned dog from the fete, and you have to admit, Sir, the drawing looks remarkably like you.'

'Rubbish,' said Sneaky Snodders taking out his hanky and blowing his long nose, while at the same time trying to tuck his long ears under his hair. 'Could be anybody. Anyway, I was at the school in my official capacity the other day. The boy could have seen me then.'

'That's true,' said PC Coats.

'Have you got a big black car?' Charlie asked.

'Here, I'll do the questioning if you don't mind. Do you have a big black car, Sir?'

'Yes,' sighed Sneaky Snodders. 'Along with half the population of this country. What has that got to do with anything?'

Charlie nudged Constable Coats, and pointed to his drawing where he had put in the car's unusual registration number.

SNE AK 1.

'Can we see the car, Sir?'

'Certainly, though I don't know what you think that will prove. It's been in the garage ALL afternoon.'

Sneaky Snodders opened the garage door, and showed them his big black car. But it wasn't the car they were interested in. It was the car's unusual registration number

**CHAPTER TEN**
*Well done, Charlie*

The following Monday morning there
was a special announcement at assembly.

There was a great cheer, especially from
Charlie.

The person responsible for letting that large black dog ruin the fete, has owned up and has... ahem... agreed to pay for the damage that was done, and also to have our roof fixed so that we can all stay at Grey Towers.

HOOOOOOOOOOOOOOORRRRRRAAAAAYYY

Mrs Tait smiled. 'As a little reward, we are giving Charlie a special new box of paints so he can carry on with his super art work. Will you come up and get it, Charlie . . . Charlie?'

But Charlie wasn't listening. He was smiling to himself at the thought of having helped save the school.

Charlie was really happy now that the school had been saved. Now he could go back to normal. Now he could go back to gazing out of the window.